Now, Now
Brown Cow!

First published 2010
Evans Brothers Limited
2A Portman Mansions
Chiltern Street
London W1U 6NR

British Library Cataloguing in Publication Data

Moorcroft, Christine.

Now, now, brown cow!. -- (Twisters rhymers)
1. Children's stories. 2. Stories in rhyme.
I. Title II. Series
823.9'2-dc22

ISBN: 9780237542566

Printed in China.

Editors: Nicola Edwards and Bryony Jones
Design: D.R.Ink
Production: Jenny Mulvanny

TWISTERS
RHYMERS

Now, Now
Brown Cow!

Christine Moorcroft and Tim Archbold

Evans

Brown cow says, "Now,
I'm going to town.

I shall powder my nose...

...and put on a gown.

I shall spend this pound
that I found
on the ground."

The owl frowns.

The hound growls.

The little mouse
runs out of the house.

Then the farmer gives a shout!

"You are not going out!

21

I shall not allow...

...a cow
to go to town.

So now,
cow,
go and lie down."

Brown Cow flounces
into the house
and on to the couch.

"Ouch!" howls the farmer's wife.
"Ouch! Ouch! Ouch!"

Twisters Rhymers follow on from the success of the **Twisters** series. Twisters are gripping short stories from different genres, told in just 50 words, with an appealing choice of illustration styles and content. Why not try one?